By: Arthur W. Hoffmann, Ed.D.

Illustrated By: Lynn Morgan

Let's have fun!
A Hoffmann
12/25/2013

Text Copyright: Arthur W. Hoffmann © 2003
Illustration and Character Copyright: ASK Publishing, L.L.C. © 2003
Song, Lyrics & Recording Copyright: Lynn Morgan © 2003

ASK Publishing, L.L.C.
1091 Centre Road, Suite 260
Auburn Hills, MI 48326

Requests for permission to make copies of any part(s) of the book or song score and lyrics for educational use will be positively reviewed and given priority consideration.

ISBN : 0-9742967-0-8

Library of Congress Control Number: 2003108529

BISAC Subject Heading:

JUV017010

Juvenile Fiction Holiday & Festivals–Christmas

First Edition

Printed and Manufactured in The United States of America
By:

Millbrook Printing Company
Grand Ledge, MI 48837
www.millbrookprinting.com

Copies of this book may be ordered by mail or by E-mail from the publisher directly,

but try your bookstore first.

Visit us on the web: www.askpublishingllc.net

Or visit the Blue King: www.blueking.net **or E-Mail him:** blueking@blueking.net

Author's Dedication:

This book is dedicated in honor of my parents to whom I owe unending gratitude for the values they stood for, practiced and instilled in our family. This story is also a tribute to Teddy Bear, my loyal companion who I will always miss.

Sincere thanks to my family and friends for their encouragement and support. Special thanks to Carolyn, daughter Kim and all my friends at TEAM Resources.

I believe it was prophetic that the gifted Lynn Morgan and I first met at an art fair on that rainy day in June 2003.

—AWH

Artist's Dedication:

Illustrating this book and writing the song and music "The Blue King" was a joyful experience.

My recently deceased parents, Frank and Leone Morgan would have found this book to be a treat for their great grand children. I dedicate this book to them for helping me see life as a gift from God.

It was great working with Arthur and Carolyn Hoffmann and the ASK Publishing team. Their creative efforts have brought a new and exciting story to children everywhere.

—LM

THE BLUE KING

Words, music and arrangement by Lynn Morgan ASCAP, Copyright © 2003

There is a place only children know
Down near the South Pole you must go
It's a kingdom all colored in blue
Come dream with me and you can go there too

Led by a man we call the Blue King
His hope is peace, that's why we sing

(Chorus)
Blue King, Blue King, teach us your way
Of sharing love with others today
With heart and soul you've taught us to give
So in friendship and harmony we can live

The King and his Queen live in a castle high
Steeples rising to the blue blue sky
Shaggy dogs and rainbows and hills of snow
Beautiful blue skies wherever you go

Oh Blue King take us for a holiday ride
Through your kingdom so mystified
You must be inspired from Heaven above
To lead a kingdom so filled with love

(Chorus)
Blue King, Blue King, teach us your way
Of sharing love with others today
With heart and soul you've taught us to give
So in friendship and harmony we can live

Now morning has opened my sleepy eyes
Somehow my world has bluer skies
Last night I discovered a land and a king
Where children all over the world will sing

(Chorus) Twice ————-
Blue King, Blue King, teach us your way
Of sharing love with others today
With heart and soul you've taught us to give
So in friendship and harmony we can live

The Blue King

Words & Music by
Lynn Morgan
ASCAP

4

Once upon a time *there was a very special child whose fascinating discovery would bring happiness to little girls and boys all around the world. This is the story of how it happened.*

Kim could not sleep. She tossed and turned in her bed most of the night and then finally drifted into a deep slumber. Her day had been filled with thoughts of tomorrow and how important it would be to her, especially if she made a mistake or did something wrong and embarrassed the Mightykicks. After all, this was the championship game and everybody would be watching her. Kim was the only girl on the soccer team and they were counting on her "big surprise." The boys called her Bluebird because the team uniform was blue and because she ran so fast that it seemed like she was flying. Kim always used to beat the boys in a foot race no matter how long the course. Not only did she run very fast but she could also zig and zag so well that they could never catch her, unless of course, she let them. Even though Kim was on the team, Coach Penny did not want to over expose her and therefore would let her play only if they really needed help to win a game. Kim would stay in the game only long enough to make sure they did win. Kim was the Mightykicks "secret weapon"—and they wanted to keep it that way.

The Mightykicks soccer team was the best team in the Junior League. They were the state champions with a record of 49 wins and no losses; they had never lost or tied a game since the team joined the league. Now for the first time in the history of Junior

League soccer, there was to be a regional playoff between the top two Central States'

champions. The winner of that game would advance to the National Championship

competition. Tomorrow—Saturday morning—everyone in the City of Rochester would

be up early, staking out their claim to the best seats and locations to watch this

important game. Soccer moms and dads from all over the state would arrive in their

vans, SUV's, trucks and some in cars, to see the exciting event. Even the visiting Central

States' champions Rockets would bring their own cheering section. Parents, friends

and family members from both teams would all gather and tailgate before the event.

Kim dreamed on, wondering what it would be like to play in the big game. Would

she do okay? Will the Mightykicks win? What if they don't? What will the coach think?

Will the boys blame her if they don't win? What will her brother Steve think?

After all, he was the one who taught her how to play soccer. Steve was a really good soccer player, but Kim could run faster. Actually that's how she got on the team in the first place. Kim remembered how her brother had introduced her as their "secret weapon." Of course Steve knew how good a runner Kim really was. Steve believed no one on the other teams would take her seriously because she was a girl. Kim thought of how some of the opposing soccer players laughed and smirked when they saw her in the Mightykicks' uniform. However, after these all-boy teams lost the game they refused to believe they were beaten by a team with a girl player. As a matter of fact, none of them ever admitted why they really lost. Players on the other teams always had an excuse like, "I tripped or fell down because the grass was so slippery," or, "She's so small I didn't want to hurt her." Once the captain of the losing team said: "We let the Mightykicks win because we felt sorry for them because they got stuck with a girl player and a girl coach."

What people did not know was how Kim learned to run so fast and to turn so quickly. Well, she owed it all to Teddy. Teddy Blue Bear is her dog. Teddy is a Bearded Collie sheepdog. He has lots of hair, even over his eyes. He really does look like a

teddy bear. He was born with blue eyes and a blue nose and that's why he was named Teddy Blue Bear. When Kim was a very little girl she liked to play with Teddy and she used to run after him and try to catch him; but she could never catch him. Of course, Teddy Bear is a natural sheep-herding dog. He can stop on a dime and reverse direction on the fly—even with hair covering his eyes. The poor sheep have no choice but to obey the dog's directions. Kim wished she could run like Teddy and one day she asked, "Why not?" Every day thereafter, Kim followed Teddy everywhere and tried and tried to keep up. She would run and turn and sometimes vault like a gymnast to imitate her teacher dog. After a while, she got so good that she could keep up with Teddy Bear.

Then one day Kim was watching Steve and the other boys play soccer at school. Well, as things sometimes happen, the boys chose sides and there were not enough players for the same number on each team. Steve's team was one person short, so Steve suggested to the other boys on his team that they ask Kim to play on their team.

At first everyone laughed and hooted, but they asked her anyway. Kim agreed to play but she didn't know all of the rules. So on the opening kick, Kim caught the ball and ran all the way down the length of the field to the opposing team's net and threw the ball in past the goalie. Everyone laughed. But Steve's teammates realized that no one on the other team was able to catch her. "Man is she fast," said one of the boys. And that is how the Mightykicks' secret weapon was discovered. All the boys agreed to help Kim learn the rules of soccer and practiced with her until she became really good at every position. She was by far the fastest player on the team. Kim also practiced on her own every day and became a very good shooter and blocker. Nobody could keep up with her when she dribbled the ball down the field. That is why Coach Penny made Kim the Mightykicks' secret weapon and decided to use her only in special situations. In this way the other teams would not know what to expect when she came into the game at a critical time. Coach Penny kept Kim on the reserve list so that the coaches of the other teams would think she was only a backup player and not very good at that. After all she was a girl trying to play a boys' sport. Other people would think she was probably there because of her brother anyway.

The Big Game

The day of the game was a beautiful Saturday morning in October. The spectators jammed the stands and the infield was filled with the early arriving parents, family members and friends. Teddy Blue Bear was the Mightykicks team mascot and he also had his own place on the sidelines. Teddy was really handy to have around because he would retrieve soccer balls that went astray. He could herd a soccer ball just like he could herd sheep. The Mightykicks had never lost a ball since Teddy joined the team. The funny thing was that everyone wished Teddy were human so that he could play for the team. Wouldn't it be great if a soccer player could run like a sheep dog?

It was late in the second-half and it had been a very exciting contest with the teams evenly matched. The game was tied with two goals each for the Mightykicks and the

Rockets. With only five minutes to go, the Rockets had the ball and they were moving quickly down the field. Everyone was excited and the Mightykicks were very worried. They might lose their first game and this was for the regional championship. Suddenly, Coach Penny decided to send in Kim to substitute on defense. Kim ran in to replace Tony, the Mightykicks best defensive player. The fans went crazy. What a dumb thing the coach was doing! Was Coach Penny out of her mind? The Rockets' fans started laughing and jeering at the bad mistake the Mightykicks were making. Buster, the Rockets' best shooter was driving on the goal and made a powerful shot at the net. As Kim entered the game she sped toward Buster and deflected the shot with her leg. Steve was watching the action and recovered the ball as it bounced around. Reversing direction, Steve dribbled the ball towards the Rockets' goal with amazing agility. But the Rockets' defense stiffened and Steve was cornered. Then he spotted Kim crossing toward the Rockets' goal. Steve had been practicing to "bend" the ball like Beckham,

the British soccer star, and instinctually kicked the ball directly to Kim, on the opposite side of the field. To everyone's amazement, the ball curved around the defending Rockets' players and Kim received the pass and drove for the goal. Steve shouted to Kim, "cook-it, cook-it" as she approached the Rockets' goalie. Kim thought of how her dog Teddy Bear would sometimes stop on a dime and reverse direction to avoid being caught. She instantly decided to try it and it worked, she caught the goaltender flat-footed. With a mighty kick she "cooked" the ball so hard that it went into the goal and tore through the netting at the back. The soccer ball then bounced a few times and started to roll. The Mightykicks' fans went wild; horns and whistles sounded. **Then a funny thing happened!**

The Adventure

As pandemonium broke out hardly anyone noticed what was happening on the soccer field. Kim was really scared because the ball she kicked broke the net and she might get blamed for kicking too hard. Could the referee give her a penalty? She wondered.

The ball was still rolling and it might even get lost. Kim then dove through the hole in the net and chased after the ball. Steve saw what was happening and followed Kim. Teddy knew it was his job to get the ball so naturally he took off after the ball, too. The soccer ball kept rolling and rolling. Kim, Steve and Teddy kept running and running after it. Steve thought that it was a good thing that the soccer ball was black and white, so that they could see it. The three of them, Teddy, Kim and Steve, kept running and running, chasing the ball. Then all of a sudden it started to get cold. And then colder and colder. The ball kept rolling.

It then started to snow. At first it was a gentle snow, but the snowflakes became bigger and bigger and more and more of them came down. The snow was almost like

an umbrella
over their heads.
It became harder
to see the soccer
ball now, but it kept
rolling on. As they
chased it, the ball started
to get bigger and bigger
and soon became a large
rolling snowball. It was easy
to follow the ball now because
as it got bigger it started to cut a
groove through the snow. Kim, Steve
and Teddy were running as fast as they
could and finally when they had almost
caught up to the snowball, the ball started going
downhill. As the snowball gained speed the kids
and Teddy Blue Bear slipped on their butts and slid
after the ball. The ball kept rolling and gaining speed making a path like a bobsled run.
Suddenly the kids heard a loud "whoosh" and then they were sliding out of control
while twisting and turning down the snowball's path faster and faster. They couldn't
even see because there was nothing but white snow. Teddy started barking and Kim

and Steve grabbed onto his tail since he was in the lead. Then they saw it. There was a bright blue light in front of them and it was getting closer and closer. "Shaboom," they were now flying through the air and in an instant they landed in a very soft snow bank. It was very quiet and everything was colored blue, even the snow. Teddy started running in circles like he was trying to catch his tail. Kim and Steve were speechless. Finally, Kim asked, "Where are we?" Steve replied, "I don't know." This place was really strange: everywhere they looked there was blue snow and the sun was shinning brightly. But it wasn't cold. Actually it felt nice and warm. "Kim, I think we're lost," said Steve. "What should we do?" asked Kim. "Well, we can't stay here," said Steve. So the three of them started walking down the hill.

Teddy Bear led the way, chasing little blue birds as they walked along. It was almost as though the bluebirds were showing the kids the way to go. Pretty soon they reached a path that led to a winding road. After a while they could see what appeared to be houses in a valley at the base of a mountain. Actually it looked more like a village. As the children reached the village they found nobody there. All the shops and houses were empty. "Where is everyone?" thought Steve. Also, another strange thing was that all the houses and shops were painted blue. As they walked around the village they saw

a large sign on the billboard in the middle of the village square which read, Hear ye!, Hear ye! All citizens must attend the King's town hall meeting today at high noon at the castle on Blue Mountain. The King summons all subjects to be present to hear a royal decree of utmost importance to all people. Kim and Steve read the notice and decided to follow the winding path up to the castle at the top of the mountain.

The Town Hall Meeting

As Steve, Kim and Teddy approached the castle they could see a large gathering in the courtyard in front of a beautiful blue castle. Soldier knights were on guard at the castle gates. The guards were dressed in blue uniforms and all of them carried large books under one arm. Everyone seemed to be very happy and they were waiting for the King to appear. The kids got as close as they could to the front gates where they could hear, but not be seen. After a little while trumpets sounded and the King appeared on a large balcony in the front of the castle. The King and his beautiful Queen were dressed in blue velvet outfits with gold trim. They each wore a magnificent crown with the words "Blue Kingdom" spelled out in colorful jewels on the bands of the crowns. The King and

16

Queen were a very distinctive couple. The King then waved to his subjects and moved

to the balcony railing where he could address the people. The crowd went silent. And

the King spoke; "My dear citizens of The Blue Kingdom, I have some very important

news for you. This morning I received a message from my dear cousin Nicholas at the

North Pole. As usual the "sea-mail" (C-mail) message came in a water-tight capsule and was delivered by Cecelia our messenger seal. Once again, Cecelia made the trip from the North Pole to our South Pole in record time carrying this important C-mail message in the capsule around her collar. However, we have a big, big problem and I need your help to solve it. There is a self-destruct lock on the message capsule and I do not know the combination to open it. In order to open the lock I must have the answer to a special riddle. The palace guard and royal staff has looked everywhere and cannot find the answer. They have searched all of our library books without success. We even tried to find the answer using all of the search engines on the world wide web and even they were stumped. We must find out what is in Cousin Nicholas' special message. Now, I want all of you to put on your thinking caps and try to help us solve this riddle."

The Riddle

The King picked up the megaphone and said, "Please listen very carefully to the words of the riddle. The whole kingdom is depending on you, the citizens of the Blue Kingdom, to solve this mystifying riddle. Here is the riddle: **What kind of a bow is it that no person can tie or untie?**" All of the people looked very puzzled. No one

spoke. "Does anyone know the answer?" the King inquired. "Just shout out if you do! Think hard my dear people, talk among yourselves. We desperately need your help." "We don't know," shouted several of the people. The crowd then became silent and all of the townspeople had sad expressions on their faces. Everyone wished they could help their esteemed King. The King was also surprised that none of the citizens knew the answer to the riddle. The King then promised a special prize to anyone who could solve the puzzle. But no one knew the answer. **What was the King to do?**

Kim, Steve and Teddy were hiding near the great castle gate behind some ever-blue bushes and heard the whole announcement. Steve said, "I wish I knew the answer, but I don't." Kim thought about it for a long time and then she broke out into a broad smile. "What is the matter Kim," asked Steve? "I know it! I know it! I know the answer to the riddle," said Kim. "You do?" exclaimed Steve. Steve then turned to Teddy Bear and said, "Kim's sure smart." "What should I do?" asked Kim. "Tell the King,"

said Steve. "Let's just all jump up and yell to him," suggested Steve. "By the way what is the answer?" asked Steve. "I'm afraid to tell the King because if I'm wrong, he might get mad at me," said Kim. "Look Kim, we're lost in a strange land, we have no food, nowhere to sleep, and they don't even know we're here. What do we have to lose?" remarked Steve. "Let's just tell the King exactly what happened to us and maybe he'll help us," said Steve. "Besides maybe we will win the prize," Steve said grinning. "All right let's do it," said Kim.

The three of them got up and ran to the gate. Kim yelled, "I know it! I know the answer!" "Who was that?" the King responded. The King peered down at the strangers. "Who are you and where did you come from?" the King shouted. "Guards, seize them. Don't let them get away," ordered the King. The palace guards dropped their books and grabbed the children. Teddy took off running and nobody could catch him. He zigzagged and ran in circles and figure 8's, herding the guards and the people into one corner of the courtyard. Then he growled and barked as his tail kept wagging and wagging. "Teddy, stay!" Kim shouted. Teddy did as he was told; he stopped and stood on his haunches facing the people like the champion show dog he really was. "Guards, bring the children into the castle so that I may talk to them. And give the dog a bone," the King directed.

The Meeting at the Castle

The King was seated on his throne next to the Queen when the children were escorted into the great hall. "Now, first things first," said the King. "Do you really know the answer to the riddle?" "Yes, I do. At least I think I do," said Kim. "Well we will find out soon enough when we try to open the capsule," said the King. "But introductions are in order first," said the King. "Now tell us who you are and how you got here," inquired the King.

"My name is Steve and this is my sister Kim and our dog is Teddy Blue Bear." "Teddy Blue Bear?" replied the astonished King. "Now that's a name after my own heart," said the King. Everyone in the great hall chuckled. Kim and Steve then related the story of the "big soccer game" and how they arrived in this wonderful but strange land. The King thought about this for a long while, and finally said, "Welcome to the Blue Kingdom."

"I am the King of The Blue Kingdom. My charges simply call me "The Blue King". We are located at the tip of the South Pole where it is very cold and very warm all at the same time. My subjects are very fortunate people. They pay no taxes and only work when they want to. We never get younger or older. Actually, we don't even know what age we are and we really don't care. We are the happiest people in the universe. Nobody has ever left our kingdom. No strangers have ever visited us, until now.

"Now, we must really get back to the riddle. Do you really know the answer? If you do, now is the time to tell us." Steve replied, "I wish I knew, but I don't. Kim does though." "Well Kim, it appears that you are the star of the moment, so what is the answer to the riddle." "Your Majesty, first you must promise that my dog, Teddy Bear, is alright and that we will get safe passage back to our Mom and Dad and our home in Rochester," insisted Kim. "Oh, we can do better than that. I will order my palace guard to escort you back to your family and pledge to you that we will always have a special place in our hearts for you, Steve and Teddy Blue Bear. I promise that no harm will come to any of you. Also, you are welcome to come back to visit us at any time as long as it does not interfere with your studies at school and your parents agree. And don't forget you will have won the special prize that I promised to whomever solved the riddle." So Kim smiled brightly and replied, "The answer to the riddle is a **rainbow.** "No person can tie or untie a rainbow." "**Eureka!**" shouted the King. "Kim, you are truly the wisest little girl I have ever had the pleasure of meeting," praised the King. "Now we must go and open the message capsule."

The Message from the North Pole

The Blue King and Queen escorted the children down the winding stairway to the castle vault where all the valuables of the kingdom were stored. The King then went over to a wall of bookcases, removed a large leather-bound book, pressed a hidden button, under the shelf where the book had been; a secret door opened which led to the safe.

The King then summoned three security guards to unlock the safe. Each guard only knew one number of the combination and the direction in which to turn the huge knob. Also, they were blindfolded so that each did not know who the other two were. One by one the guards approached the King and whispered the combination number and direction to him. The King turned the dial to that number and then that guard left the vault. When all three numbers were entered the King himself dialed in his own special number and the safe opened. Every day the combination was changed for security purposes. Steve and Kim stared wide-eyed at the many treasures inside the safe. On a pedestal under a glass dome was the message capsule from the North Pole. The King then ordered the electronic security and surveillance devices turned-off while he removed the capsule. The King then closed the door of the safe and had the security devices turned back on. Kim and Steve followed him to a table in the vault room where he carefully set down the capsule. The shining silver capsule contained a keyboard for punching in letters and numbers, just like a computer. "Now we shall see if Kim is right," said the Blue King as he gave a most peculiar laugh. This was the first time the King had laughed out loud. He wrinkled his nose and laughed, **"Hee-Hee-Hee-Hee!"** Well, with that the King handed Kim the capsule, and asked her to open it using the answer to the riddle. Kim was very nervous and her hands were shaking. And then she started to cry. "My dear, what is the matter?" asked the King. Kim replied, while sobbing, "I know the right answer, but I'm not sure I can spell rainbow and I don't want to make a mistake." "That's okay Kim, I'll help you," said Steve. And the Blue King laughed, **"Hee-Hee-Hee-Hee."** Kim looked at the capsule's keyboard and

then punched in the letters that spelled **R A I N B O W** on the keyboard. For a moment nothing happened, but then a loud buzzer sounded and the top of the capsule popped open. The King removed the rolled-up message and read it very slowly. And then he read it again. "This is great news," he exclaimed! "What does it say?" asked Kim and Steve in unison. "It is good news for the Blue Kingdom and all of its citizens," remarked the King. "Come, I must tell all of our people."

The Proclamation

The Blue King and his court assembled in the "Great Hall" that was filled with all of his subjects including the townspeople. The King and Queen sat on their thrones, while Kim and Steve sat in huge blue velvet high back chairs. And Teddy Bear had his own blue velvet cushion, which was specially made for him by the Queen's seamstress. At the sound of trumpets the court herald pronounced to the gathering: "Loyal citizens of the Blue Kingdom, Hear Ye! Hear Ye! This court and its subjects are convened for the purpose of receiving a proclamation from our beloved King. All bow to the King." And everyone did. The Blue King rose from his throne and saluted his subjects,

"My dear people, I have good news for all of you. With the help of our young visitors from the North we were able to solve the mysterious riddle and open the message capsule from my Cousin Nicholas, at the other end of the globe. As you know, he and his elves are very busy, especially at a certain time of the year. Saint Nick, as some people call him, loves all girls and boys the world over. And he does his very best to bring happiness to all of them. But, every year his gift lists get longer and longer and his sacks get bigger and bigger. Fortunately, he is able to enlist more and more volunteer elves and helpers so he can continue to do what he does. Cousin Nicholas is so busy he has to work every day, all year round just to get ready for his one-night delivery job. However, my cousin has often told me that during his hectic travels all around the world that he has come to recognize the need for all people everywhere to help and assist their neighbors in any way they can to make the world a better place. Since we the citizens of the Blue Kingdom have no other worldly commitments, I, on behalf of the citizens of the Blue Kingdom, volunteered to sponsor a special program to help girls and boys to grow up to be special young adults.

"So recently, I sent a C-mail message to Cousin Nicholas proposing that we, the citizens of the Blue Kingdom, establish a special humanitarian mission to bring about peace and understanding among all people. Since children naturally like other children, no matter who they are or what they look like or where they come from, they would make ideal ambassadors of good will. The goal is to encourage all boys and girls to always practice **F**riendship, **U**nderstanding and **N**iceness to all the other children they meet. We would call it our **FUN** program. Every year our 'Blue Kingdom'

monitors will scour the globe to find and recognize deserving children who have demonstrated friendship and understanding and have been nice to everyone they have met. Our Blue Kingdom monitors will then select these nice children and recommend that Cousin Nicholas deliver a special present, wrapped in blue, to acknowledge their contribution to making the world a better place. In this way, these special children would make their mothers and fathers very proud. And the world will be a better place. In his special C-mail message Nicholas replied that he was thrilled when he received our proposal and thought it was a grand idea that was so much needed and so long in coming. Cousin Nicholas also said he would be honored to deliver the Blue Kingdom special recognition gifts along with his other regular delivery orders."

"Therefore, on behalf of all the citizens of the Blue Kingdom, I am announcing this proclamation."

Proclamation: "By order of the King of the Blue Kingdom I proclaim that from this day forward the Queen and I as well as all citizens of the Blue Kingdom will dedicate ourselves to bringing about Friendship, Understanding and Niceness among all of our neighbors the world over.

Our motto will be: Let's have FUN. Every citizen of the Blue Kingdom will be an official FUN ambassador."

All of the citizens of the Blue Kingdom then cheered with approval at what their wise King had proclaimed.

The Ceremony

The Queen smiled and rose to address the crowd. "My dear subjects, this has truly been a grand day. In honor of this wonderful occasion I wish to invite all of you to share in our happiness by joining the King and me and our gracious visitors at a gourmet banquet in the castle this evening." Many of the townspeople had never been inside the actual castle or in the banquet hall so this was indeed a special occasion. The excited crowd clapped and cheered and quickly left to dress up for the gala event.

That evening the cheerful and anxious citizens—dressed in their finest—lined-up and filed through the castle entrance. They were then guided into the great banquet hall where they were seated at the long tables facing the King and Queen and their honored guests. Teddy Blue Bear, of course, was lying, on his special pillow, under the table at Kim and Steve's feet. At one end of the hall there was a huge aquarium, which was the home for the messenger seals. Cecelia and her family were frolicking on the ice glaciers. The other seals and penguins wiggled and waddled on the ice or swam very gracefully for all to see. Roving musicians and jesters entertained the people. After a while a scrumptious meal was served. People would later say, it was a meal fit for a king. When dinner was over the herald announced that the King wanted to say a few words to his subjects and to make a special presentation.

"My dear subjects and honored guests, I wish to thank all of you for your support of the FUN project and your continued allegiance to the Blue Kingdom. From this day

forward you will all have the official title Ambassador of the Blue Kingdom. You will travel far and wide in support of FUN. You are to identify and sponsor any and all children who do good deeds in their daily lives and practice FUN. You are to find and recommend deserving children whom you feel should be rewarded with a special gift. Cousin Nicholas will deliver this gift on his special night during the joyous holiday season. Of course, the names of the children you pick must be kept a complete secret until the special day. In order to make sure the list of names is kept secret we will lock the list in the castle safe until it is needed. And you all know how difficult it is to open my safe. **Hee-Hee-Hee-Hee,**" the King giggled.

"I have another important announcement to make. Dear Kim and Steve it is my great pleasure to appoint you as Honorary Citizens of the Blue Kingdom, with all rights and privileges the Kingdom can bestow. You are also appointed Ambassadors of FUN. The Queen and I are also very pleased to proclaim Teddy Blue Bear the honorary mascot of the Blue Kingdom. The Queen and I are so very **grateful for** …….."

Let's Have Fun

Suddenly Kim heard a voice calling her. "Kim! Kim! Kim dear please wake-up. It's Saturday morning and you and Steve have a big game to play," said Kim's Mom as the alarm clock chimed. "Where am I?" Kim awoke with a start. "Mom, you'll never believe what happened to Steve and me. It was so real." Kim pinched herself to make sure she was awake. "Kim, dear you must have been dreaming. I hope it wasn't a bad dream?" asked her mother. "Oh no, Mom, it was a very good dream but it didn't feel like a dream.

29

I will tell you all about it later," said Kim. "Right now I have to get dressed, eat breakfast and get ready for the big game. I sure hope Steve is ready too." "Oh, Kim I almost forgot to tell you that this letter came for you this morning." Kim's mother was holding a blue envelope in her hand. Kim grabbed the envelope and tore it open. In the blue envelope was a note on blue paper that simply read, "Good Luck in your game today! And remember to have FUN. **Hee-Hee-Hee-Hee.**" The note was signed with the symbol of a crown. Kim grinned from ear to ear. "Mom, please make sure you bring Teddy Bear to the game today. I have a strange feeling we may need him," remarked Kim.

The Beginning, not the End!

Blue King Request

To all parents, grand parents, caregivers and people of goodwill the World over.

The Blue King invites you to be an ambassador of **FUN**. His Majesty requests that each of you encourage our children and young people to demonstrate Friendship, Understanding and Niceness to everyone they meet.

The Blue King asks that you support this humanitarian effort by recognizing deserving children (and any others you love) by rewarding them with a special gift during the holiday season or at any other appropriate time for practicing **FUN**.

Signed by The Crown

FUN Application

I _____ want to be a FUN Ambassador and
your name
help the Blue King to bring Friendship, Understanding and Niceness to everyone around the World.

I pledge to do my best to treat everyone I meet with friendliness and respect no matter who they are or where they come from. I want my Mom and Dad to be proud of me. I hope to be selected as a special person by FUN volunteers and I am looking forward to receiving a special gift during the holiday season that will be delivered by Saint Nicholas (Santa Claus).

Signature or mark: _____

C-mail to: blueking@blueking.net   **Please visit the Blue King @**
                                                      www.blueking.net

Or snail mail to: The Blue King
                      P.O Box # 570
                      Saint Clair Shores, MI 48080

Fold & Seal

Your Return Address

Name _____

Street Address _____

City & State _____

Zip & Country _____

| Place |
| stamp |
| here |

The Blue King
P.O. Box # 570
Saint Clair Shores, MI 48080